MW00464951

To Hell
and Back

TO HELL
AND BACK

A STORY OF
REDEMPTION

PETER EGGLETON

atmosphere press

© 2021 Peter Eggleton

Published by Atmosphere Press

Cover design by Kevin Stone
Art by Valeria Knakhovskaya (lera.knah@gmail.com)

No part of this book may be reproduced without permission from the author except in brief quotations and in reviews. This is a work of fiction, and any resemblance to real places, persons, or events is entirely coincidental.

atmospherepress.com

FOREWORD

I was very touched when my young friend Samantha actually asked me to write a foreword to her account of a recent visit to Hell. Although the great majority of people who 'visit' here don't go back, you might be surprised how many do. But I suppose that most of them are too traumatised to write a decent description, and many of the rest are too inarticulate. In addition, although I not infrequently call people here for a cautionary interview, it really doesn't seem to teach most of them the lesson that I try to get across, and they are probably too embarrassed to reveal that.

I know Samantha won't mind my saying that it was my suggestion she rewrite her account in the third person, rather than the first person. It makes her account seem a bit more objective, a bit more sophisticated, a lot less air-headed. I also helped – *entre nous, beaucoup* – with the grammar. What do they teach young people in California schools these days?

I'm very glad that Samantha has been able to capture some, at least, of the hi-tech aspects of our operation here. We are pretty proud of our leadership role. Not many people realise that a lot of the electronic gizmos they waste their time with were invented here. I can recall whispering a few ideas in young Bill's ear back in about 1975, I think, and *voilà*, Microsoft! And the telephone answering machine with the endless circuit of menus to choose from: a masterpiece, though I say it myself.

Orpheus and Dante were two of the earlier people to visit here and write about it, but neither of them asked my opinion about their writings. I'm not complaining, but I thought Dante gave a rather labored account. At least, however, he managed to convey something of the vibrant energy here, as compared with Paradise. But I think he had a few axes to grind. As for Orpheus, although I love the can-can, I can't really see its relevance.

Someone who captured some of the essence well, even though he never came here himself, was Mozart. I *love* the bit where the voice of the dead Commendatore summons Don Giovanni down to Hell! I've used that a few times myself, subsequently. And whenever I start humming that tune about the party he's going to throw, *Finch' han dal vino*, I can't stop. Oh dear, there it goes again, *tum titty tum tum, tum titty tum tum, tum titty tum tum, tum titty tum!*

Now I won't be able to get rid of it.

Goethe, Schmoethe! I think the man was obsessive-compulsive, or perhaps anal-retentive. We're not down on people like Dr Faustus looking for knowledge, we're actually rather for it as I indicated above. What we don't like is the abuse of wealth and power, particularly by dirty old men. I think Samantha's narrative gets that point across rather well.

Ciao, darlings.

Hell, 1 iv 2009

Chapter 1
Samantha meets Abdul

'She's dead? I hope she goes straight to Hell!'

No sooner had Samantha said this than she felt bad about it. The bitch had insulted her, humiliated her, and had tried to get her fired. She was the mistress, or mistress-that-was, or perhaps the mistress-to-be, of Samantha's employer, the elderly playboy owner of the jewelry-store chain where Samantha worked. Wilbur Smith had a whole chain of stores across the country; but he lived in San Francisco and so it was to this store that he usually came when he wanted something in diamonds for his current girlfriend. Samantha had had him pointed out to her before, but this was the first time that it fell to her to carry out the transaction. The woman was haughty, greedy and tasteless; but tastelessness was just what she accused Samantha of, when Samantha reluctantly produced the only diamond brooch that anyone of quality would have been seen dead wearing. And when Samantha was a little slow to swallow the insult, the woman had turned to Wilbur and said, 'Fire her!'

It didn't help the psychodynamics of the scene that Wilbur was rather quickly and obviously taken with Samantha. He was ogling her when the woman turned to him and barked out her order. He hesitated in such a marked manner that the woman had stormed out of the shop. She stalked straight across the road outside, and was knocked down by a passing truck. Samantha's supervisor, who had been smoking on the sidewalk outside, burst in with the news that she was dead, her head crushed flat.

By this time Wilbur had already started to overwhelm Samantha with his practised charm, and had suggested she might choose some jewelry for herself. Samantha was in fact rather easy to overwhelm in this way, although Wilbur was hardly intuitive enough to pick up her inclination to sluttiness. So, her outburst on hearing the news was perhaps a little overdone. But she had hardly experienced her regret before a strange, sudden stillness fell on her. She froze; and the world about her seemed to dissolve in an instant.

She closed her eyes. She seemed to be falling and yet remaining vertical, as if in an elevator whose cable had snapped. But when the falling stopped, whether hours or milliseconds later, and apparently without catastrophic results, she opened her eyes again and found that she was standing in a completely different place, a large, red-lit room in which the light, mostly coming from behind her, flickered slightly. The room was sparsely furnished, and the wall directly in front of her was a single huge mirror. It took her more than a moment to recognise that she was seeing herself, and when the recognition hit her she could not quite take it in. She seemed to be having the kind of out-of-body experience that she had sometimes read about in the tabloids.

Although she did not feel paralysed, she seemed unable to will herself to move. Her usual response to a mirror was to preen herself. But her arms were fixed in front of her. She couldn't move her head, or even her eyes, to look and see what was holding them, but in the mirror she could see perfectly well. The sight should have terrified her, and yet it didn't – it was as if she were watching someone else in a movie.

She was still in the posture that she had been in when pointing to some brooch in the cabinet that she had been standing behind, legs apart and leaning forward a little with her hands on the cabinet. At either side of her was a creature, perhaps four feet tall, that was like a big lizard but with nearly human hands. They were standing up on their short hind legs, balanced by their scaly tails. These creatures were placing her hands, which had previously been on the display cabinet in front of her, on a horizontal rail at the same level as the cabinet and so at a little above the level of her waist. They wrapped her fingers round the rail. She was helpless; yet curiosity rather than fear was uppermost in her mind.

Then the mirror broke open: or rather, a door in it opened, and a woman stepped through, clad in a red skin-tight body-stocking. But as she approached, Samantha recognised with a shock that actually she was red-skinned and naked. From her neck up, her skin paled to much the same color as Samantha's; and with even more of a shock, Samantha recognised the face: she was the bitchy trollope.

'Your hope is realised, my dear!' she said, in an oddly warm and friendly manner. 'Hell is where I come from, actually. I'm Satan.'

There was a slight movement from something attached to the ceiling near the middle of the mirror, a bit of machinery that Samantha recognised as a camcorder, like those that watched in the jewelry store. A moment later, a disembodied woman's voice, trying to be sprightly yet sounding only lifeless, said 'Thank you for visiting Hell ... *Samantha*. This interview may be recorded, for training purposes only.' Her name was pronounced with a slightly different accent.

Even though this promised to be an unpleasant interview, Samantha still could not will herself to move, to scream, or even to faint. In a moment, Satan continued. 'Please don't worry, my dear. In an hour or so you'll be back Above. And time there is standing still, as it happens, so you'll be back without anyone noticing that you left. In fact, we're in a different set of dimensions here altogether, that connect to your Universe via wormholes. Your world Above is four dimensions, and here we're in a different four dimensions, out of the thirteen that string-theorists *ought* to be talking about'. The allusion was lost on Samantha, but Satan carried on as if chatting over a coffee table with an old friend.

'I didn't go Above to trap you, my dear. Actually, I was more interested in Wilbur Smith. He hasn't bought our product yet, but I'm rather afraid he's going to. Why on Earth should a billionaire pay with his soul for the power to seduce anybody he fancies? You would think he had it already. Yet somehow these dirty old men never have enough. I really don't understand you humans. I used to say that it's your greed that keeps my corporation in business; but in the last fifty years there's been so much greed I have difficulty keeping up with it.

'Not your greed personally, my dear,' she added as an afterthought. 'At least I don't think you're in Mr. Smith's league. Really, I brought you here to warn you.'

Satan turned aside, to one of the salamander-like creatures that had clenched Samantha's wrists around the rail and now cowered against the wall to one side. 'Go and fetch Abdul, Beelzebub. He's not far behind that door there.' There was no apparent door, but the monster pushed against the wall and a gap opened. For a moment the light of flames flickered, and wisps of smoke with a sulfurous smell trickled through. Then the gap closed.

'I want you to meet Abdul. He's one of our employees here. He works 24/7, poor devil – there's no trade union here. But maybe once a month I give him an hour off, because he works like a demon.

'Abdul is a bit like you, though you may not think so when you first see him. He's really a sweet guy, a pussy cat. But he did something rather awful, in a fit of anger, shortly before he was killed, and so he was contracted to a thousand years of employment here. He's an ECO – Extreme Correctional Operative. He's done nearly six hundred years already. Don't tell the Board I give him an hour off each month,' she winked conspiratorially, 'or they'll give him another eighteen months'.

The door opened, and a man appeared. He was a huge, muscular man built like a gladiator, and yet he had a miserable, beaten-down look. His once-white tunic was stained with blood and mud, as were his arms and legs. His hair was matted. One eye hung from its socket; the other was bloodshot.

In one of his hands was an arm, a woman's arm. Blood

dripped from tendons at one end. 'Throw that back, Abdul,' said Satan testily. He obeyed, and closed the door, though not before another whiff of sulfur burst out.

'Abdul, you look awful,' said Satan, 'And you smell awful too. Go and take a shower'. The man stumbled slightly as he made for a door in the wall at the end of the mirror. There were two doors close together there. Samantha could see that one door said 'Ladies/ Gentlemen/Demons'. The other said 'Monsters'.

'Abdul was a slave in the harem of a Prince,' remarked Satan. 'He belonged to one of the Princesses. He should have been a eunuch, of course, but the Princess pulled a fast one over the harem-master. She switched Abdul for his twin brother, who *was* a eunuch. Abdul's job was to pleasure his Mistress, when the Prince wasn't doing it. And that was most of the time, because the Prince preferred, er, boys.'

She broke off for a moment. 'Don't get me wrong. We're quite indifferent here to sexual orientation. I know you're from San Francisco; you needn't feel uncomfortable here.'

Then she continued, 'Abdul loved his work, and so did the Princess. But a new slave girl took a fancy to him too. In a fit of jealous rage – instantly, bitterly regretted, I might say – she told the harem master. That bastard, with four soldiers, overwhelmed Abdul, and chained him to the wall in the guard room. He ordered the guards to rape the princess – they were eunuchs, of course, but you'ld be surprised what some eunuchs can do – and then he tore out Abdul's tongue, and one of his eyes. But Abdul, bless him, with the strength of a giant, broke his chains, and he tore that man's head right off with his bare hands. Then he went after the soldiers, all four of them, and killed them all. But the Princess was already dead, poor soul; she died of shame – well, a heart attack.

'No reason to send Abdul to Hell, you might think. But then he went after the slave girl. Of course, it was her fault, but she was heart-broken. She begged him to kill her at once. But he tore off her arms and broke her legs; she didn't actually die for two days. By that time Abdul had bled to death internally – one of the soldiers had managed to spike him with a dagger.

'It was a very difficult case for our Inhuman Resources Committee to adjudicate. I would have let him off if I'd been chairperson, as I often am. But I was on foreign travel, and he was sentenced to a thousand years. The girl, I might say, got two thousand; she works in another department.'

Abdul emerged from the shower room, and certainly looked a lot better. He smelt better, too, having evidently found some Imperial Leather talc. He had bound up his eye with a strip torn off a towel. His posture was now vibrant, erect, and since he was naked Samantha could clearly see that his prick was too. It was gigantic.

'Well, I mustn't keep rattling on,' said Satan. 'Abdul deserves a break; and you, my dear, deserve a lesson. I think, I hope, you're just a slut, and being a slut isn't the sort of sin that will get you here – not permanently, anyway. The lust for money, for power over others, the contempt for the poor people that you can lord it over, and that make your lifestyle possible; selling your soul for that kind of power, that's what gets you here *for ever*. And as I was saying to Woody Allen the last time I saw him, "for ever" is a long time, particularly towards the end.'

Despite her promise, Satan kept rattling on. As Abdul approached Samantha, Satan said, 'I think you'd better go *behind* her, darling. That eye is a bit off-putting, at least on a first date.' Then she added, to Samantha, 'Don't worry, my dear, he's not a sodomite. Pleasure is what Abdul likes giving, not pain; which is why he really deserves a break from time to time.' When Abdul was close enough to touch Samantha, Satan snapped her fingers, and a tube appeared in Abdul's hand. Samantha recognised it as a tube of KY jelly, in the economy size. 'It'll hardly hurt at all,' said Satan; 'You won't feel a thing'. And as Abdul passed behind her, she got a whiff of mint. He must have had time to brush his teeth. Samantha was thankful; if there was one thing she couldn't stand in a man, it was the smell of bad breath.

Abdul made some effort to remove her underwear, but there was little he could do except rip it apart, which he did with such controlled strength that she felt only the frisson of cloth against skin as the cloth fluttered to the ground. The fornication did hurt at first, but nothing like as much as Samantha expected; and towards the end she found in spite of herself that she enjoyed it, and furthermore was quite unable to conceal the fact from Satan's close scrutiny.

Satan clapped with glee. 'You really did it, girl!' she said. 'I'm going to recommend to Inhuman Resources that Abdul get two hundred years off his contract.' She added, to Abdul, 'Do take her hands off the rail, dear boy.' Abdul complied. Then Satan dismissed him with a gesture, but before he left she gave him a clean tunic from a cupboard.

Chapter 2
How Hell Works

With another gesture, a chair appeared, and Satan waved to Samantha to sit down. Samantha pushed down her skirt, before sitting down rather gingerly. 'Don't worry about the torn underwear, my dear. My people will fix that as you fly through the wormhole back to your Universe. Hell is a bit like las Vegas: what happens here, stays here. And, by the way, that also applies to the possibility of, er, babies. You don't have to worry.'

Samantha had noticed that she was no longer unable to move, but she found that she still couldn't speak. Satan, however, didn't seem to need any response. 'You're wondering about our organisation here, I know. And how a big boss like me can find the time to talk to a little person like you.' Samantha didn't take offense, because that was exactly what she was wondering. 'Like any CEO, I have to be in a dozen places at once, but unlike most CEOs Above that's what I actually *can* do. I can be male as well as female, too. I can even fuck myself, if I want to, but I'm usually too busy. I bet you wish your supervisor could do that.

'We have customers here, and we have employees – very different categories. The customers are people who've bought our product, wealth and power, paying with their souls, for eternity. Most of them, poor dears, didn't realise they really do have to pay. But here in Hell, the customer is always wrong, you'll be glad to hear. The employees are nicer people, actually. Usually they did something wicked and regretted it. Poor people who stole to keep their families alive hardly count: they might do a year or two. Abdul, as you've gathered, is an employee, an ECO. He was a bit more wicked, but it was a hot-headed, spur-of-the-moment thing, and he regretted it before he died. There are actually a lot more ECOs than customers. But the employee turnover is very difficult for our organisation: even a thousand years is a lot shorter than *for ever*. The job of employees, for the most part, is to punish the customers, and it's no fun – particularly for the salary.' She snickered. 'Abdul, of course, has to tear off arms and heads, and even sometimes legs, which is really hard work.

'You're wondering how damned souls can have their arms and legs torn off in perpetuity, but then you don't know about our health plan. I call it Satancare. Our ER people can sew arms and legs – and even heads – back on, and in a month or two they're as good as new. It's much the same for customers who are being skinned alive, or boiled in oil. Some of our oldest customers are chained to a rock, and have their livers pecked out piece by piece by eagles – they're mostly left over from classical Greece. But our biotech department is wonderful: they can reconstitute liver from eagle shit and re-implant it.

Satan explains Satancare to Samantha

'And just like Above, our health plan covers the rich and the powerful, the *customers*, first; the little people come last. ECOs like Abdul are right at the end of the queue, I'm afraid, but I really hope he'll get his eye fixed quite soon. His tongue might take a bit longer.'

She paused, and patted Samantha's knee. 'You've learnt a lesson, my dear, at least I hope you have. You felt sorry for Abdul, not right away but quite soon. You saw someone worse off than yourself, and you did something nice for him, to relieve his distress. All right, you enjoyed it in the end, but you didn't expect to, at first. Enjoying doing someone a favor is OK: doing well by doing good, I call it. Just provided the doing good matters more to you than the doing well. Of course, Above it's often hard to tell – you have all those hucksters and hot gospelers clamoring for your money. Here in Hell though, we read people's *souls*.

'Well, strictly speaking a customer that gets here hasn't got a soul, because they sold it or they wouldn't have got here. But potential customers – not you, dear, at least on this occasion – are searched by Immigration Department agents before they get here, and they have to pass by the soul-detectors at the entrance. Those detectors used to be infallible, of course, when they were angels; but they were replaced by computers. Someone on our Board of Directors got a backhander from Microsoft, and so we had a lot of bugs, and people had to go through a dozen detectors sometimes before we could get a reliable diagnostic. I pressed for Linux, and we finally got them; but by then the Board of Directors had made a dozen tests mandatory. So, we not only waste a lot of time and money, we end up with much more work in Hell because a lot of people who haven't actually lost their souls lose them while waiting in line for check after check.

'People who do still have some soul, but it's been a bit damaged by bad thoughts or actions, get routed to the Employment Department, like Abdul. Of course, some people have such unpolluted souls that they go straight to Heaven. I doubt if you've met many of them though; they're not usually buying jewelry inside jewelry stores.

'You heard me say I'll get two hundred years off Abdul's contract. I think you've already figured out that if you come here twice more, he'll be free – he'll go to Heaven.' She paused again, and then added, 'Of course, he'll be re-united with his Mistress, the Princess. If that makes you jealous, then I'm sorry for you. In Heaven, they can fuck all the time; but it's a kind of mind-fuck. Actually "fuck" is much too crude a word for it. It's more like telephone sex.'

She moved her hand, and a cellphone appeared in it. She snapped it open, and pressed a button. 'Oh, *darling*,' she trilled, 'I can't wait for you. I've been playing with myself all day, thinking of you.' She opened her thighs, and slid her other hand down. 'Are you ready? You're not? Well, fuck off.' She giggled, as the cellphone disappeared again. 'It's a lot better than that in Heaven. But it's abstract, and my fingers would be playing with a harp.'

Samantha had begun to feel more comfortable, but comfort turned to embarrassment for a moment as she saw that Satan was now a lot more absorbed in herself than she had appeared to be. 'Playing' became working for a short while; but after a few minutes she sighed, closed her eyes and relaxed. 'I haven't done that for ages,' she said. 'I'd forgotten how good it feels.'

'You're thinking, why don't I get Abdul to fuck me, whenever I want? Well, the Board really discourages affairs between the senior staff and the junior employees, and of course I have to set an example. Affairs could lead to all sorts of unfairness. Fairness and unfairness is what it's all about here.

'A lot of people misunderstand our work. We don't *try* to get souls, we've got too many already. The product jumps off the shelf! If there were no more need for this organisation, I'd be the first to resign; I'd get a pretty good pension, don't worry. In fact, like all those CEOs from financial institutions Above, if I get laid off for any reason, then it's in my contract that I get a golden handshake that's worth thirty times my salary. But I'm old-fashioned, I want to do this job *well*, even though it gets harder and harder, with a flood of new customers every time some government deregulation allows the fraudsters more leeway.

'Once upon a time, just after we were taken over in a hostile bid by the Christians under Emperor Constantine, we were instructed to go out and tempt sinners. But after fifty years we were so overwhelmed by rich and powerful Christian bishops that we had to backtrack. Nowadays the bishops aren't so awful, just the odd bagman for the Mafia, and a few paedophiles, but the level of greed in the laity seems to never stop increasing.

'Of course, we've got a lot of big financial people here. This particular department – where Abdul works – is the Infernal Revenue Department. Tax cheats come here; not everyone who ever told a lie on their tax return, but those who made a habit of it, and thought that it showed how clever and important they were. They knew perfectly well that the "little people" would have to pay extra because of it, but despised them for being so little and stupid and honest. Abdul works in the Ladies' Department, which is even bigger, you might be surprised to know, than the Gentlemen's. Well, there are so many rich widows; their husbands made the money, and now the widows spend it. An awful lot of them feel it's unfair for them to be taxed at all, can you believe it?

'Since we were privatised, in the Reagan era, I've had mission statements sent down to me by the Board that are always telling me to punish more people, and harder – but they never give me the resources to do it. I don't know how we're going to cope with just the Savings and Loan aftermath, let alone Enron, once those people are ready to come here. We'll need to construct a whole new building, and getting new resources from the Board is like getting blood from a stone. And please don't even *mention* the recent financial meltdown. I just can't imagine where I'm going to put them all.

'That nice Mr. Madoff isn't down here yet. I hope he won't get here for a few years, because we're going to have to build a penthouse suite for him. I'll have to do some creative accounting to fund it, but maybe that won't be too difficult following all the deregulation that's gone on. We've actually got two Jewish blocks here in Hell, one for Orthodox and one for Reform. Most Reform Jews don't actually believe in Hell, and that has a pretty bad effect on morale there: the demons are full of self-hatred, and the building is very badly maintained. The Orthodox building is beautifully clean, and the demons there take a lot of pride in their work. But I suppose Madoff is Reform, so we'll have to put his penthouse on top of that pile of junk.'

A signal beeped on Satan's computer, and a woman's voice, unnaturally even-toned, said 'Bernard Madoff is Orthodox, I think'. 'Oh, thank you Siri', said Satan, sounding more than a little sarcastic. 'That's really useful.'

'You know,' she continued, 'US politicians *love* Hell. It allows them to sound tough on crime, without costing anything - well, anything much. We get a subvention from the FBI, laundered through so many accounts that actually *nobody* knows where the money's coming from, or going to. The politicians, oddly enough, are convinced that Hell doesn't apply to *them*. They assume they can blarney or bribe their way out of it. I love the look on their faces when they find that they can't!

'Anyway, nowadays what I try to do is *prevent* people buying our product. We are bound to run at a loss: just the price of sulfur, for instance, not to mention natural gas – and now oil! – ruins our bottom line but the Board expects me to minimise the loss. We've tried laying off employees, but even I can't make the remainder work more than 24/7. Anyway, we don't save much money by layoffs, since the ECOs aren't paid.' She snickered again. 'All we might save is on Admin costs, and there's never much saving there in practice because Admin decides how many administrators we need, and we always seem to need more – and pay them more.

'You will have seen, I'm climbing out on a limb in trying to get Abdul released early; but it's a matter of fairness, and I think you saw that he really is such a *sweet* guy. If I can have you persuade Wilbur Smith not to buy our product, then I can let Abdul go early. Of course, the Philandery Department is quite different from Infernal Revenue, but we encourage retraining – "career enhancement", it's called.

'Do you realise just how sweet Abdul is? He doesn't know the slave girl got two thousand years, and I'm not going to tell him. I just *know* he would beg me to let him do two thousand years more, and let her go. That's how nice he is.

'So it's up to you. I want you to persuade Wilbur to leave his money to charity – a proper charity, that helps really poor people in countries you've never heard of. I'll email you a list of *real* charities, not ones where the officers pay themselves and then spend the rest of their money soliciting more. Wilbur is going to die soon, of a heart attack, so you've got two to three months. I'd like you to come back here in a month, and again in two months, to help poor Abdul. And in the meanwhile, I'm trusting you to help us out by steering Wilbur away from us. Try to see that he doesn't sell his soul for easy fornicatory success, at least. And better still, if he regrets having got rich off the sweat and blood of those poor people in Africa, digging and being murdered for his diamonds, he might end up here as an ECO, instead of as a customer, and that will help us a lot. Ask him about 'blood diamonds', for instance. I know you've heard of them, and I'll put a website address in that email, for you to read as well as Wilbur, a website that's really up-to-date. Things change quite rapidly there. Of course, Wilbur's got to *genuinely* regret the harm he's done, not just try and buy a little good feeling. You may not be able to recognise which it is yourself, but you won't be blamed for failing if you *try*.

'Come to think of it, it might be a good idea for you to persuade Wilbur to visit one of the places in Africa where his diamonds come from. I think some of them are relatively safe nowadays.

'Well, I must be going. I'll have IR write a contract. You'll be a Flex-Time employee, which means we can fire you any time, not a Full-Time Equivalent ECO like Abdul, who can only be fired if he enjoys his job. The paperwork will probably take a month. Bye-bye!'

Chapter 3
An Excursion to Africa, and its Cause

Wilbur Smith pulled himself a little further under the shade of the thorn bush. He ached all over. One of his arms hurt so badly that he supposed it must be broken. Mud and blood stained the safari suit that he had bought with such insouciance at the airport when they arrived. In the shade the flies were less bad, as well as the sun. He didn't know if he had the strength to get up, but at least he wasn't dead.

Samantha, with the interpreter and the driver, had gone on in the jeep to locate the next town. He had stayed in this village, hoping that his little French might allow him to communicate. This was the sort of village which the Banque Populaire d'Afrique was supposed to help, with micro-loans to the villagers. Wilbur was impressed with the small but neat plots behind each hut, where the women grew vegetables. A ten-dollar loan from the Banque allowed them to buy fertiliser. The interpreter had told him that the fertiliser had doubled the crop. With any luck they could sell their excess produce for twenty dollars, repay the loan with 6% interest, and still have a little to save. Those who repaid their loan – and that was in fact all of them – could expect to borrow more this year, supposing they could break some fresh ground to cultivate. They were saving up for machetes and spades to clear a scrubby patch, the very patch that Wilbur was lying in.

It was probably lucky for them all that they had not yet got their machetes. A gang of four hooligans, agents of the robber baron who had seized the diamond mine nearby, had stormed through, looking for children that they could enslave. The villagers had to run, carrying their children. If they had had machetes they could hardly have used them, their arms full of children, and the hooligans would no doubt have seized the machetes and made the fullest use of them. Fortunately, this particular gang seemed to be from the bottom of the totem pole: they had no weapons themselves, just sticks and fists, and they were malnourished and scrawny to the point of emaciation.

In his youth Wilbur had been a boxer, even winning a belt at Yale. It was many years since he had fought, and never in anger. His heart condition meant that he even had to be careful climbing the stairs. At the memory of this he felt a sharp pain in his chest; but it passed away. His breathing had slowed to its usual rate.

He and three other men had stood and fought. Wilbur knew he would have a heart attack if he ran fast enough to escape, so he thought he might as well die fighting. The other men were presumably saving their extended families. Wilbur saw no sign of them. A couple of the hooligans, in their torn green shirts, lay in the dirt ten yards away; the other two must have fled. He hoped the two lying there were dead, otherwise they might get up before him and beat him to death.

He remembered the screams of a young woman that three of the hooligans had tried to rape. That was when Wilbur had stopped thinking about his heart, and started using his fists. She had run like the wind, her dress half torn off. He hoped she had escaped.

There was the sound of talking, getting nearer. Women's voices were among them so presumably the villagers were returning. Soon someone saw him, and there was excited chattering as several crowded round. Wilbur found himself dragged out by his legs – not his arms, thank God – and groaned and turned over.

The villagers seemed delighted that he was still alive. One woman, whom he recognised from her torn skirt as the one nearly raped, leant over him, wiped his face, and swatted away some flies. Then two men helped him to stand. They took him by the arms, and since he didn't have to scream he knew they couldn't be broken.

A little group led him gingerly over to one of the huts. Among the group was one of the men who fought, he was glad to see. This man must have fared better than Wilbur; he didn't seem to be injured. Most of the group then took themselves off, leaving him in the care of the woman and an older woman. Wilbur guessed that they were mother and daughter.

Laughing and smiling, they pushed him gently on to a bed, just a piece of canvas on top of something he judged to be straw or leaves. The younger woman started stripping off his clothes, and wiping away the dirt with a wet cloth. The older woman fetched something from a cardboard box.

It was a bottle of beer! Grinning, she wrenched the top off with her teeth. She only had three teeth, but one of them at least must have been strong, and in the right place. Laughing and chattering, but in a patois Wilbur could barely understand, she gave him the beer. Wilbur knew that in the last town beer was 50 cents a bottle, and he realised that this must be five per cent of the woman's annual income. But she pushed it into his hand and gestured to him to drink it.

The beer was warm, but Wilbur had had worse in London. It went down his throat like a ferret down a rabbit-hole. Not so much from the alcohol, he supposed, but rather from relief, he felt almost light-headed. He stopped worrying about whether the damp rag he was being washed with was sterile – at least his skin did not appear to be broken, though some bruises were already showing darkly. Presumably the blood came from his attackers. In less than five minutes he was falling asleep; but he had a strange sensation as his eyes closed that a hand that had been unfastening his trousers was now stroking his prick. So comfortable was he that he felt none of his usual anxiety about the smallness of his member. Once upon a time he would have sold his soul for a proper-sized prick. He had been told as a schoolboy that seven inches was average, and no amount of straining would make his more than five and a half. Through half-closed eyes he saw the older woman's grinning face, fat and round, scarred on one side, with her three teeth showing in a grin that seemed to illuminate the entire hut. As he lapsed into sleep he felt as comfortable as a baby being sung to by his mother.

It had taken some prompting – nagging, perhaps – on

Samantha's part to get Wilbur to come to Africa, indeed, to spend any time thinking about anything except getting her knickers off. But Samantha had a strange attraction for him. Most of his girls were after his money, or jewelry in lieu. Generally, in a month or two they got what they wanted, and he got what he wanted. Except that he never got what he *really* wanted, because it wasn't there to be got. Yes, some of the girls might say, 'Ooh, it's *huge*', but it was clear to Wilbur that they were at best being kind; at worst, they must be laughing behind his back, the bitches. Samantha had refused jewelry. The very first day that he saw her, he thought he had seen her eyes light up in the acquisitive way he was used to. He was amused by her hasty invective when someone rushed in to the shop to announce that Wilbur's latest mistress-to-be had been killed by a truck. Wilbur was not hard- hearted, but that woman had been nastier than most. As Wilbur responded by suggesting that Samantha might choose something for herself, she had been strangely silent for a moment, even a little startled. But when he got her attention again, she merely said, in a rather abstracted way, 'I don't want a necklace, I need a drink.'

Common decency required that they stand outside for a bit, part of the throng that had collected, until an ambulance had departed with the remains. Wilbur spoke to the police, who might have been giving the driver a hard time but was relieved to find that already several witnesses had described how she had strode straight across the street without looking. There was no crosswalk here, in the middle of the block.

Then Wilbur tried to steer Samantha to the bar of the St Francis Hotel, but she insisted on Starbucks instead.

Coffee was apparently the drink that she needed. She had been quite silent while Wilbur went through his usual spiel about how nobody had ever looked prettier. Then, when he paused for a while, she said quite carefully, but without any apparent malice, 'Are you sure the diamonds you sell aren't blood diamonds from Africa?'

This didn't entirely take Wilbur by surprise. You couldn't live in San Francisco without being beaten up by liberals from every direction. He said, cautiously, 'We do get them certificated, my dear.'

'Is that foolproof?' she demanded. 'If I thought a single diamond in that shop of yours is a blood diamond, I'd quit right away.'

Wilbur was quite sharp enough to see the sincerity of her concern. 'I believe it is,' he said, 'But I'll have my people check.' Then he added, in a moment of unusual insight, 'Did you see that program on the History Channel last month? I must say I hadn't quite realised how dreadful things are. Perhaps I should check it out myself. I've been *told* that things are a bit better now, in Africa.'

'I did see it,' Samantha said, 'though it hadn't quite gotten through to me till very recently. Someone told me about a website to read, that's up-to-date. I think I'll go home and read it. Would you like to come too?'

She was cautious enough to look in at the shop. Her supervisor was minding the till. She looked daggers at Samantha, but she also recognised Mr. Smith and practically curtsied. Yes, it must have been quite a shock, so Samantha could have the afternoon off. She would get her own back later, some way, somehow.

Samantha's invitation to him to join her in her apartment took Wilbur a little bit by surprise. He had expected her to play hard-to-get but she didn't. There was something a little impersonal about the way she started to masturbate him almost as soon as they were sitting on the couch, and then she mounted on his lap and rode him, her knickers pulled to one side, until he was satisfied a few minutes later. It wasn't clear to him if she was satisfied herself – it never was, to Wilbur – but at least she didn't overact her pleasure as some girls did. Her only comment was, 'My, it *is* stiff!' and he was comfortable with that because it really was about the stiffest it had ever been at least since he was a schoolboy. She seemed somehow to generate an absence of anxiety, in opposition to his usual experience, and anxiety was a terrible antaphrodisiac.

Then she turned to her email. She was relieved to see no conspicuous message from satan@hell.com, but a rather less obvious sheila.tan@multiverse3.net. 'Sheila Tan is someone I know at my Rhythm and Motion dance workout class', she lied easily. Wilbur and she took turns reading about the progress of diamond certification, and watching videos shot by an intrepid reporter.

The reporter took them on a trip through two villages that had recently been freed by UN soldiers from the grip of the local robber baron. There was something unexpectedly heart-warming in seeing how the villagers were picking up their lives again. 'I *do* wish I could do something to help them,' said Samantha.

Then she turned to the list of charities that Sheila Tan recommended. There were only five, and mostly they sounded like rather boring banks. The one thing that they had in common was small loans to individuals. There was even a note in Sheila's message, when Samantha got around to reading it more carefully, to avoid the sort of grandiose schemes for building four-lane highways or airports. These did more good for American investors in big corporations, and for the corrupt megalomaniacs who ruled some African countries, than they did for the suffering poor.

When they had finished, Samantha announced, 'I'm going to put my savings into one of those banks. They pay 5%. I call that doing well by doing good.' Then, although it was only the middle of the afternoon, she took off her clothes and drew Wilbur to the bedroom.

Chapter 4
Hell Revisited

Exactly a month to the second after her outburst in the jewelry store, Samantha found herself back in Hell. Although she had expected it, she had somehow forgotten during the last ten minutes, while she had been playing with Wilbur's member. So, when she found herself back in the interview room, she saw herself in the mirror kneeling, her thighs wide, but with no one between them.

No salamander-like monsters were attending her this time; at least, they were not directly attending to her, but as she looked around she saw them huddled by the door of their room. Her capacity to will herself to move seemed restricted, but not so much as before; she felt as if she were swimming in treacle as she continued, for a moment or two, to squeeze and stroke a non-existent prick. Wilbur had been doing extremely well.

A door opened again and in came Satan. This time he was male. He was about six inches taller than his female *alter ego*, and with a much broader torso, and an impressive musculature. He was naked as usual, apparently, but his genitalia were relaxed and unobtrusive. His tail, however, was much more conspicuous – Samantha had barely noticed it on her previous visit. 'You've been doing very well, my dear,' he said. 'I'll call Abdul.'

When Abdul emerged, he was as dirty as before. There was no woman's arm in his hands this time, but if anything, he looked even more down-trodden. And this despite the fact that his eye had apparently been replaced. Both were bloodshot.

Satan evidently sensed the pity that Samantha could hardly conceal. 'It's not the arm-pulling that gets him down,' he remarked, 'it's the paperwork. You have no idea.' Abdul went again to the shower room, and Satan continued. 'Abdul is a bit intellectually challenged, as you've probably guessed. It's a real effort for him to fill in those forms. He couldn't even read and write when he first came here, but he went to some training classes. Now, after pulling off an arm in five minutes, it takes him an *hour* to fill in the form. And of course, they change the form every decade, just when he's getting used to it. It never gets shorter, only longer. The HMO people need name, crime, injury, medications they're allergic to, Social Insecurity Number, Heaven knows what else. You'd think they had it on file already. Many of the customers have been here for ages, I mean *ages*. And they've all got their SINs branded on their backsides, so it seems quite pointless.'

'Talking of paperwork,' Satan continued, 'I haven't yet got that contract back from IR. They lost the first lot of papers, and the second lot has only been with them a week. I'll check later, but don't worry about it, all it really does is make sure that whatever goes wrong, it's your fault and not ours.'

Abdul was much improved, as before, when he emerged from the shower. His eyes even looked less bloodshot, although it might have been a trick of the light. He gave Samantha a lovely smile – perhaps a little tight-lipped, a little Mona-Lisa-like, but he probably didn't want to show his mouth too much. Satan clicked his fingers to get the attention of the two monsters. 'Beelzebub, Melchisadech, fetch that trolley from your room'. The two salamanders, who had been cowering by the door of their lair, fetched from it a leather-covered contraption, resembling a sort of gurney that patients are moved around hospitals on.

At Satan's bidding, Abdul lifted Samantha up, as easily as a child, and laid her on it, rolling her carefully so that she was face-down and central. She still had her tights, knickers and bra on, because Wilbur found women's underwear erotic.

Rather than tear off her bra, as she expected, Abdul struggled with the clasp, until Samantha took pity on him and did it herself. Her knickers followed quite easily, although still with Samantha's help. But the tights were a problem; perhaps Abdul had never seen tights before. He solved the problem with his usual finesse, ripping them in two. Then he stood for a few moments admiring the unfamiliar material, holding it up to the light, and grinning through it.

Satan stood a tube of cream on the trolley near Samantha's face. It was called 'Crème de Beauté: Cashmere Mist', but it was made in China. 'Abdul loves to give massage,' said Satan. 'This will do your skin good. It's been checked for lead, beryllium, vanadium, arsenic and ruthenium. It's below the FDA maximum for children's sweat and blood. Last year it would have been above it, but fortunately the Board relaxed the criteria and now we can use our old stocks. So, bye-bye – I'll be back, but for now I really have to vanish'; which he did.

Abdul began to rub the cream on her, starting at her neck and shoulders and working his way slowly downwards. Although his hands were powerful, she could tell from their tenderness how much he enjoyed this work. For her, it was like being fucked all over. He turned her over gently and massaged her front as well. By the time he was finished, first massaging and then fornicating, both of them were well content.

Not long after, Satan reappeared, and this time she was a woman again, though with a different face. 'I really hope your contract isn't through yet, my dear, otherwise you'll have to write a report,' she said. 'But it's obvious you've earned Abdul another two hundred years off.' She was probably referring to drops of semen on Samantha's belly, with a trickle running down her slit. 'I'll give them a call.'

She gestured to Abdul to sit down. He did so, but not before picking up the remains of Samantha's tights. He seemed happily absorbed in stretching them this way and that, looking through them and sometimes kissing them.

Satan picked up her phone, and pressed a button. She must have left the speaker on, because a voice said quite clearly 'Your call is very important to us. Please select from the following 15 options'. They were largely incomprehensible to Samantha, but Satan evidently chose one, and a different voice said much the same, offering ten more options. But after Satan's selection of one of them, instead of still more options a voice said, 'Please wait fourteen minutes for the next available demon.' And some music came on, which Samantha recognised as one of her favorites, Vivaldi's Four Seasons.

Satan beamed broadly. 'I love Vivaldi. He worked here for a few years, maybe ten. His sin wasn't very big, thank goodness. He was a priest, but he had an affair with a nun, a singer in the Cathedral's chorus. It wasn't abuse, they really loved each other, and he helped her career as a singer'. Satan was clearly in an expansive mood, as she sat through several rounds of 'Your call is very important to us; please hold on'.

'Even the people whom he was boiling in oil appreciated him. I recall one Pope telling me he'd rather Vivaldi manage the fire than anyone else – he was so musical. Always whistling a tune, never the same one twice. I expect he's doing that in Heaven now – whistling, I mean, not boiling oil.' Finally someone came on the line. The voice was in a foreign language, but the discussion was short. Satan put the phone down and said 'As I expected, it's not ready yet. You're in luck.'

'About Wilbur,' said Satan, after a brief pause. 'I checked our files. Wouldn't you know it, someone had misfiled his report. It seems as though he wasn't thinking of selling his soul for easy conquests. Apparently he's suffering from SPS – Small Prick Syndrome. That's a tough one. Is his prick really small?'

Samantha was at a bit of a loss. She felt it was necessary to be scrupulously fair. 'It's not as big as Abdul's,' she started. Satan laughed: 'Nobody's is! But how is it compared with average?'

'I'm not sure I know what average is,' said Samantha. 'I know Wilbur thinks the average is seven inches, because he told me so. But apart from Abdul, I've never seen one that was over, maybe, six inches.'

'The average for Caucasians is 5.4 inches,' said Satan. 'And it's not much larger for Afro-Caribbeans, whatever anyone says or thinks. The standard deviation is about 0.8 inches. There was an article in Lancet a few years ago. They measured several thousand. What a dreadful job that must have been.'

'You know,' she continued, 'there's a lot of anecdotal, contra-scientific bullshit around. It's a question of self-appraisal. Like, 95% of people think they have an above-average sense of humour. If you read the self-assessment reports of our ECOs, as I have to, you'd know that 90% of our ECOs are performing above average. I wouldn't be surprised if 99% of men are afraid their pricks are small. And at the same time, I bet that 50% of women think their tits are too large and 50% think they're too small. If you were one of our SCOs, you would qualify to apply for an LDRD grant to investigate that.'

'What's an SCO? And what's, er, LDRD?' asked Samantha. 'Sorry dear, SCO is a Supervisory Correctional Officer. It's a step above ECO, for people whose souls are only slightly damaged. And LDRD is Libidinously Directed Research and Development.'

Just then, a buzzer went off on Satan's desk. Satan looked at her watch and said 'Oh Goodness, I've forgotten something. Please excuse me – I won't be a moment.' She was as good as her word; a moment later she was back, but entirely changed in appearance. She was back to being male again, rather prominently, and naked except that he was covered from head to foot in gold foil apart from his horns which were large and silverplated.

'Sorry about that! Today is Friday the 13th, in case you didn't notice. Every Friday the 13th, I have a little meeting with a few of the corporate oligarchs that run America. It's usually in an old, ruined chapel in New England. I like to have them dance around me, holding hands and chanting something. Today it was "Trickledown, trickledown, ha ha ha!" Then they licked what trickled down my legs.' He looked uncomfortable for a moment, and glanced down at his legs, but then he gave a little sigh of relief and added, 'Well, they seem to have got rid of it, thank Goodness. I wouldn't want to embarass you'.

Satan continued, 'Talking of trickledown economics, you might be interested to see some of our recent work here.' He led her to a door in one side wall. 'We're building a wall here, ostensibly to keep out attempted immigrants from the shithole territory to the left. I really mean "shithole"; the people on the other side are trickledown-supporting economists, and the corporate oligarchs who fund them, who are being boiled in vats of shit. Of course they want to break through, or climb over, this wall so they can be boiled in vats of oil instead, which is a lot pleasanter as you can imagine.' As Satan spoke, an emaciated figure dropped down from the top of the wall; two of Satan's minions grabbed him, and hurled him into the nearest oil-filled vat, where he started laughing with relief. 'He'll qualify for Satancare much sooner here,' said Satan laconically. 'But it's time for you to get back. Have Wilbur read that Lancet article – I'll email it to you. I really think it could save his soul, though you've been doing a great job in that direction yourself.'

'And, by the way, don't be alarmed by the odd sensation as you go back Above. Last time, you looked a little startled. Time runs backwards, but very quickly, as you fly through the wormhole. You'll be rapidly unfucked, but I'm told it's quite a nice feeling when you're used to it.'

Chapter 5
A Charitable Donation

Wilbur was not as rich as Samantha, the gutter press, and even Satan had supposed. A couple of divorce lawyers had creamed off most of his money, and he was down to his last fifty million. But he was now determined to join Samantha in funding a bank that would make microloans to the sort of villagers he had met in Africa. And he had gone through the diamond certification process with a fine-tooth comb, uncovering in the process some corruption in the office of de Bores, and some other suppliers.

After much discussion, in which Samantha played the Devil's advocate, Wilbur decided to give his money to the poor: not just leave it as a legacy, but actually give it. At least, he would give it to the five banks, who would lend it to the poor. The reason for this was partly practical. His will might be challenged by lawyers, and even if he 'won', the money would all disappear; but they could hardly challenge his giving it during his lifetime. Could he trust these banks? – a difficult issue. On Samantha's urging, he sounded a few people he was fairly sure he could trust: the Dalai Lama, Warren Buffett and Prince Charles, for instance. The Dalai Lama's list was just the same as Sheila Tan's, and the others overlapped quite considerably.

So Wilbur found himself penniless, and he moved into Samantha's little apartment. Samantha got him a job in a coffee house round the corner, one that purchased its coffee beans directly from small producers in Costa Rica. She was sadly aware that he didn't have long to live, but she hadn't told him of Satan's prophecy. Besides, Wilbur really knew it himself; his heart had been playing up a bit more since his fistfight in Senegal.

Since learning that his prick was of average size, or even a tiny bit more, his morale had improved a lot. Samantha kept him sexually active, developing an extraordinary repertoire of foreplay, play and afterplay that kept him busy when he was not waiting at the coffee tables, so he hardly had any need for money. The only thing that sometimes handicapped his performance was when he remembered the dreadful scenes on video of people with their limbs hacked off by brigands in search of blood diamonds. 'I'm so ashamed of myself!' he would weep. 'I should have known it was happening.'

Whenever she could, Samantha would cuddle him, and gently play with his prick until he fell asleep. This wasn't as often as she would have wished, because her malevolent supervisor kept finding excuses to give her some unpaid overtime. Nevertheless, it was often enough to earn Wilbur's dog-like devotion. It was on just such an occasion, when Wilbur had Friday off, that Samantha found herself back in Hell for the third and last time.

Chapter 6
Abdul released

'I'm really proud of you,' said Satan. He was spiffed up in a tuxedo, and apologised for not having had time to undress. He had been to a Hollywood film launch, and babbled on for a minute or two in a rather self-important manner about the celebrities he had met. He had been searching for sincerity, but had been unable to detect it.

Abdul, after his shower, was more cheerful than ever. His smile was wide, and he could hardly stop himself from licking his lips. Evidently his tongue repair work had finally been done.

There was no hospital trolley this time, but at Satan's semaphored order the salamanders dragged out many floppy cushions from their lair and made a pile of them. Abdul carried Samantha to the pile and laid her gently on top of it, the small of her back on the uppermost cushion. She was wearing a short frilly nightdress, something that Wilbur had helped her choose from the Victoria's Secret catalog. Samantha had formerly been accustomed to sleeping naked, at least in company, but Wilbur really liked to have a present to unwrap. The nightie was apparently not short enough for Abdul, however, since he carefully ripped the hem apart and then tore the front open all the way up. The Princess must have had an awful lot of clothes, she thought.

He stood back a little, and admired Samantha's body with an unselfconscious smile. Then he knelt near the edge of the pile, eased Samantha's legs wide apart, and gave her a kiss on her *mons veneris* that seemed full of pent-up longing. Gradually he put his tongue to work, searching out nerve centers that even his careful massage had missed before. Samantha knew a little, of course, about her clitoris, but she never knew as much as she learnt in the next forty minutes. Most of her knowledge was second-hand, in fact, and came from one of the instructors at a women's dance group she used to attend. When it became clear how interested the woman was in Samantha's own clitoris she had stopped attending.

Abdul's tongue was amazingly agile. There was no part of her vulva, and its neighborhood, that did not receive attention. He lifted her body with his hands under her buttocks, raising it as if to drink nectar from a chalice. Each orgasm that she experienced had a different edge to it, as if her body were a flute on which many tunes could be played.

At last Abdul let her rest, and he sat down comfortably beside her. Samantha's hand sought his member; it was flaccid, but soon grew in strength. When at last it erupted, a fountain of molten lava burst from it and spattered her from her face to her thighs.

Satan had been working at his laptop, but he heard

Abdul groan and looked up. 'Very good, my dear,' he said. 'Abdul's pink slip should be coming through any moment now. As a matter of fact, so should your contract – just in time for me to put it in the shredder.' It didn't trouble Samantha at all that Abdul's happy smile must be due to the thought that he would soon be reunited with his Princess; surely he deserved such a reward. A laser printer in the corner sputtered, and in an instant Abdul disappeared.

'I expect you've been wondering why the Princess went straight to Heaven, when so many of our customers here led less enjoyable lives.' As usual, Satan had read her thoughts exactly. 'Well, it's a question of intention as much as action,' he continued. 'The Princess led a very sheltered life: brought up in her father's harem until she was fourteen, she was sold to the Prince and joined his harem. I say "sold": her father paid a dowry, of course, but he got back much more in terms of power and influence. All that she ever saw of the outside world was one glimpse through the window of her litter, on the ten-minute journey from one palace to the other. In that glimpse she saw a beggar lying at the roadside, and she was so upset that she couldn't settle at first. Then that evil harem-master tricked her into believing that the beggar was a saint fulfilling some vow. How could she have known any better? Of course, if she'd been a bit brighter she might have figured out that the whole world couldn't be living the way she was living. But you can't blame people for being stupid, only greedy. She could read, as well as embroider and sing, but the books in the harem were only love-poems, embroidery textbooks and such; she never had a chance to learn of the real world. And she was nice to her slaves – didn't even realise they *were* slaves. After all, the harem slaves were living better than most of the people outside, so they weren't about to complain.'

'It's fortunate, though, that that was a long time ago, before the crowds in the Immigration lobby became so huge. I told you about the soul-scanning machines. I'm reading a report here that says that, thanks to some security scare, people who are rejected from Hell, as customers at least, because they still have their souls largely intact, now have to line up for a *second* set of a dozen machines, one after the other, to get into Heaven. It's not just a total waste of time and resources; a lot of people in this second line lose their souls before they get to the front! All the more work for us, worse luck. And fewer workers to do it, because the ones who lose their souls entirely in the second line are mostly the ones with somewhat damaged souls, who would have been ECOs like Abdul. Since our corporation got privatised, I sometimes think our Board of Directors has lost all touch with reality.'

'Of course, we're thinking about outsourcing to India. We're very interdenominational here, but the Hindu operation is separate except at Board level. They have a very economical operation: punishable souls are reincarnated into dung-beetles, or rats, or untouchables, so there's no need for ECOs. Not that the ECOs are a cost item, but we should be able to make do, you might think, without the army of bureaucrats that boss them about. Think again! We're holding a feasibility study. The preliminary paper claims it's not so effective in practice, even if it's cheap; and of course, the administrators on the committee all think it's a bad idea. For some on the Board, cheap is everything. For others, saving their own jobs is everything. I'm sitting on the fence myself.'

'Well,' said Satan, 'it's been a real pleasure getting to know you. It may sound unkind, but I really hope we won't meet again.' Samantha found herself flying back through the wormhole – and found that cunnilingus was as good backwards as forwards, though disappointingly quick.

Chapter 7
Wilbur redeemed

Wilbur had lapsed into sleep, his guilt mercifully suspended for the moment. Without meaning to, but as a result of her instantaneous adventure, she squeezed his member so hard that it woke him. Samantha straddled him, and set about riding him.

Abruptly, she cringed helplessly for a moment and then farted. It was not a major source of smell, but the sound reverberated, and Wilbur burst out laughing. 'I love you,' he cried, and then lost control. Crying 'Oh my God! Oh my God!' he practically flung Samantha against the ceiling, and ejaculated. It was not up to Abdul's standard, but Samantha was not judgmental – it was the best she had ever got from Wilbur.

Then Wilbur, after a few seconds, said 'Oh my God!' again, but much more quietly. Samantha felt alarm: Wilbur was gripping his chest, and tried twice to sit up, falling back each time. Then, with a murmured 'I love you,' he fell back, white and deathly still.

The doctor was very understanding. 'This happens every day. I'll have to notify the coroner of an unexpected death, but you can be sure he'll be discreet.' When he had gone, the phone rang. The caller ID said, 'out of state', and a woman's voice she recognised said, 'Someone you know passed through the *second* line OK. Congratulations!'

ABOUT ATMOSPHERE PRESS

Atmosphere Press is an independent, full-service publisher for excellent books in all genres and for all audiences. Learn more about what we do at atmospherepress.com.

We encourage you to check out some of Atmosphere's latest releases, which are available at Amazon.com and via order from your local bookstore:

Saints and Martyrs: A Novel, by Aaron Roe

When I Am Ashes, a novel by Amber Rose

Melancholy Vision: A Revolution Series Novel, by L.C. Hamilton

The Recoleta Stories, by Bryon Esmond Butler

Voodoo Hideaway, a novel by Vance Cariaga

Hart Street and Main, a novel by Tabitha Sprunger

The Weed Lady, a novel by Shea R. Embry

A Book of Life, a novel by David Ellis

It Was Called a Home, a novel by Brian Nisun

Grace, a novel by Nancy Allen

Shifted, a novel by KristaLyn A. Vetovich

Because the Sky is a Thousand Soft Hurts, stories by Elizabeth Kirschner

ABOUT THE AUTHOR

Peter Eggleton is an astrophysicist who has worked in Cambridge University, UK (1962 - 2000) and Lawrence Livermore Laboratory, California (2000 - 2010) before retiring to live in Alameda, California. He has written one other book, Evolutionary Processes in Binary and Multiple Stellar Systems, Cambridge University Press (2006), UCRL-BOOK-209818, and one or two hundred scientific papers.

His insight into Hell, and particularly into the concept of Satancare, came to him when he had to spend two months in the Recovery Room after an operation for cancer in 2008.

Say hello at peter.eggleton@yahoo.com.

CPSIA information can be obtained
at www.ICGtesting.com
Printed in the USA
BVHW071205231121
622335BV00009B/303